DEAR TEDDY ROBINSON

In these eight delightful tales, perfect for reading aloud to young children, Teddy Robinson pays a visit to the Dolls' Hospital, gets stuck up a tree, pretends to be a polar bear and lots more.

DEAR TEDDY ROBINSON

Joan G. Robinson

Galaxy

CHIVERS PRESS
BATH

First published 1956
by
George G. Harrap & Co
This Large Print edition published by
Chivers Press
by arrangement with
Penguin Books Limited
1999

ISBN 0 7540 6075 6

British Library Cataloguing in Publication Data

Robinson, Joan G. (Joan Gale)
   Dear Teddy Robinson. - Large print ed.
   1. Teddy Robinson (Fictitious character)—Juvenile fiction
   2. Children's stories, English 3. Large type books
   I. Title
   823.9'12[J]

ISBN 0-7540-6075-6

Printed and bound in Great Britain by
REDWOOD BOOKS, Trowbridge, Wiltshire

CONTENTS

For
Gregory
Barnaby
Mungo
Jessamy
and everyone
who has a Teddy bear

CHAPTER ONE

TEDDY ROBINSON GOES TO THE TOYSHOP

Teddy Robinson was a nice, big, comfortable, friendly teddy bear. He had light brown fur and kind brown eyes, and he belonged to a little girl called Deborah. He was Deborah's favourite teddy bear, and Deborah was Teddy Robinson's favourite little girl, so they got on very well together, and wherever one of them went the other one usually went too.

One day Teddy Robinson and Deborah were going with Mummy to a big toyshop. Deborah had fifty pence to spend. It had been sent to her at Christmas.

'You must help me choose my present, Teddy Robinson,' said Deborah. 'It will be nice for you to see all the toys.'

'Yes,' said Teddy Robinson. 'You couldn't really manage without me.

Shall I wear my best purple dress?'

'No,' said Deborah, 'your trousers will do. It isn't a party.'

When they got to the toyshop there were so many things to look at that Deborah just couldn't make up her mind. Teddy Robinson got quite tired of being pushed up against the counter and squashed against ladies' shopping-baskets.

'Perhaps I'll have a glove-puppet,' said Deborah.

'Then put me down for a bit,' said Teddy Robinson. 'I'm tired of being squashed, and I don't much care about glove-puppets anyway.'

So Deborah sat Teddy Robinson down by a large dolls' house, and he sang a little song to himself while he was waiting. This is what he sang:

'See Saw,
  knock at the door,
  ask me in and shake my paw.
  How do you do? It's only me,
  it's half-past three,
  and I've come to tea.'

"*How dare you stare in at my window?*"

Teddy Robinson peeped through one of the upper windows of the dolls' house. A tiny little doll inside was sitting at a tiny little dressing-table. When she saw Teddy Robinson's big furry face looking in at the window she gave a tiny little scream. Then she said, in a tiny little, very cross voice:

'How dare you stare in at my window? How very rude of you!'

'I'm so sorry,' said Teddy Robinson

3

politely. 'I'd no idea you were there. I was just looking to see if the windows were real or only painted on. I didn't mean to look in your bedroom window.'

The tiny little doll came over to the window of the dolls' house and looked out.

'That's the worst of living in a shop,' she said. 'Everybody comes poking about the house, and looking in at the windows, and asking how much you cost, and wanting to come inside and look round. Well, I'll tell you now—we cost a great deal of money, we're very dear indeed, and you *can't* come in and look round, so there!'

Then the tiny little doll made a rude face at Teddy Robinson, and pulled the tiny little muslin curtains across the tiny little windows so that he couldn't see inside any more.

'Dear me!' said Teddy Robinson to himself. 'What a very cross lady! I'm sure *I* don't want to go in her house. I couldn't, anyway—I'm far too big. But it would have been politer if she'd asked me to, even though she could see I was too fat to get through the door.'

Just then Deborah came over and picked Teddy Robinson up.

'I've decided I don't want a glove-puppet after all,' she said, 'so we're going to look at the dolls now.'

So Deborah and Teddy Robinson and Mummy went to find the doll counter. On the way they passed dolls' prams, and scooters, and tricycles, and a little farther on they came to a toy motor-car with a big teddy bear sitting inside it.

'Oh, look!' said Deborah. 'Isn't that lovely!'

'The dolls are over there,' said Mummy, walking over to the counter.

'Listen, Teddy Robinson,' said Deborah, 'if I put you down here you can look at that bear in the car while I go and look at the dolls.' And she put him down close to the car so that he wouldn't get walked on or knocked over, and ran off to join Mummy.

Teddy Robinson had a good look at the toy motorcar and the teddy bear sitting inside it. It was a beautiful car, very smart and shiny, and painted cream. The teddy bear inside it was very

"Are you a shop bear?"

smart and shiny too. He had a blue satin bow at his neck, and pale golden fur which looked as though it had been brushed very carefully.

Teddy Robinson was surprised that he didn't seem at all excited to be sitting in such a beautiful car. He looked bored, and was leaning back against the driving-seat as if he couldn't even be bothered to sit up straight.

6

'Good afternoon,' said Teddy Robinson. 'I hope you don't mind me looking at your car?'

'Not at all, actually,' said the bear in the car.

'Are you a shop Bear?' asked Teddy Robinson.

'Yes, actually I am,' said the bear.

'You've got a very fine car,' said Teddy Robinson. 'Are you going anywhere special in it?'

'No, actually I'm not at the moment,' said the shop bear. 'Don't lean against it, will you? It's a very expensive car, actually.'

'No, I won't,' said Teddy Robinson. 'Why do you keep saying "actually"?'

'It's only a way of making dull things sound more interesting,' said the shop bear. 'Anything else you want to know?'

'Yes,' said Teddy Robinson. 'Can you drive that car?'

'Actually, no,' said the shop bear. Then, all of a sudden, he leaned over the driving-wheel and said in a quite different voice, 'Look here, you're a nice chap—I don't mind your knowing. Don't tell, but it's all a pretend. This car

7

doesn't belong to me at all, and I don't know how to drive it. They put me here just to make people look, and then they hope they'll buy the car.'

'Fancy that!' said Teddy Robinson. 'And I was thinking how lucky you were to have such a very fine car all of your own. You look so smart and handsome sitting inside it.'

'Yes, I know,' said the shop bear. 'That's why they chose me to be the car salesman. But it's a dull life, really. If only I knew how to drive this car I'd drive right out of the shop one day and never come back.'

'All the same,' said Teddy Robinson, 'it must be rather grand to be a car salesman.'

'What are you?' asked the shop bear.

'Me? I'm a teddy bear. Don't I look like one?'

'Yes, of course,' said the shop bear. 'I meant, what is your job?'

Teddy Robinson had never been asked this question before, so he had to think hard for an answer.

'I suppose I'm what you'd call a Lady's Companion,' he said. 'I belong

8

to that little girl over there. She isn't exactly a lady yet, but I expect she will be one day.'

Just then Deborah ran back, so Teddy Robinson had to say good-bye to the shop bear very quickly.

'You must come and see the dolls,' said Deborah. 'There aren't any nice ones for fifty pence, but some of them are simply beautiful just to look at.'

She carried Teddy Robinson over to where Mummy was looking at a very large doll, dressed as a bride.

'Now just look at that one,' said Deborah. 'She's quite three times as big as you are, Teddy Robinson.'

'And she can walk, and talk, and you can curl her hair,' said the shop-lady who was standing by.

'She really is beautiful,' said Mummy, looking at the price-ticket, 'but we couldn't possibly buy her.'

'Is she *very* dear, Mummy?' asked Deborah.

'Yes,' said Mummy, 'very dear indeed. She is five pounds.'

'Dearer than me?' said Teddy Robinson.

9

'Oh, yes,' said Deborah, 'a lot dearer than you. She costs five whole pounds,'

'Well,' said Teddy Robinson, 'if she costs five pounds I bet I cost a hundred pounds. Ask Mummy.'

'Mummy,' said Deborah, 'how much did Teddy Robinson cost when he was new?'

'About one pound fifty pence, I think,' said Mummy.

'Not as much as that doll?' said Deborah.

'Oh, no,' said Mummy. 'That doll is much dearer.'

'Fancy that!' said Teddy Robinson to himself, and he felt half surprised and half cross to think he wasn't quite the dearest person in the whole world.

'I don't think it's much use our looking at dolls any more,' said Mummy. 'They're all so dear.'

'Yes,' said Deborah, 'and I've just thought what I really would like to buy. Couldn't I have one of those dolls that are really hot-water bottles?'

'Why, yes,' said Mummy. 'What a good idea!'

So they all went along to the

chemist's department, and there they saw three different kinds of hot-water-bottle dolls. There was a hot-water-bottle clown, and a hot-water-bottle Red-Riding-Hood, and a hot-water-bottle dog, bright blue with a pink bow.

Deborah picked up the blue dog.

'That's the one I want,' she said. 'Look, Teddy Robinson—do you like him?'

"Isn't he rather flat?"

'Isn't he rather flat?' said Teddy Robinson.

'Yes, but he won't be when he's filled,' said Deborah. 'He's a dear—isn't he, Mummy?'

'Yes,' said Mummy, 'he really is.'

'Everybody in this shop seems to be dear except me,' said Teddy Robinson to himself. And he felt grumpy and sad; but nobody noticed him, because they were so busy looking at the blue dog, and paying for him, and watching him being put into a brown-paper bag.

All the way home Teddy Robinson went on feeling grumpy and sad. He thought about the doll dressed as a bride who was three times as big as he was.

'It isn't fair,' he said to himself. 'She didn't have to be three times as dear as me as well.'

And he thought about the tiny little doll who hadn't asked him into the dolls' house.

'She was a nasty, rude little doll,' he said, 'but she told me *she* was very dear too.'

And he thought about the blue-dog hot-water bottle, who seemed to be coming home with them.

'Deborah and Mummy called *him* a dear, too. But I don't think he's a dear. I don't like him at all, and I hope he'll stay always inside that brown-paper bag.'

But when they got home the blue dog was taken out of his brown-paper bag straight away. And when bedtime came something even worse happened. Teddy Robinson and Deborah got into bed as usual, and what should they find but the blue dog already there, lying right in the middle of the bed, and smiling up at them both, just as if he belonged there!

'*Look* at who's in our bed!' said Teddy Robinson to Deborah. 'Make him get out.'

'Of course he's in our bed,' said Deborah. 'That's what we bought him for, to keep us warm. Isn't he a dear?'

Teddy Robinson didn't say a word, he felt so cross. Deborah put her ear against his furry tummy.

'You're not *growling*, are you?' she said.

"*Look at who's in our bed!*"

'Yes, I are!' shouted Teddy
Robinson.

'But why?'

'Because I don't like not being dear,'
said Teddy Robinson. 'And if I aren't
dear why do people always call me
"Dear Teddy Robinson" when they
write to me?'

'But you *are* dear,' said Deborah.

'No, I aren't,' said Teddy Robinson; 'and now I don't even *feel* dear any more. I just feel growly and grunty.' And he told her all about what he had been thinking ever since they left the toyshop.

'But those are only dolls,' said Deborah, 'and this is only a hot-water bottle. You are my very dear Teddy Robinson, and you're quite the dearest person in the whole world to me (not counting Daddy and Mummy and grown-ups, I mean).'

Teddy Robinson began to feel much better.

'Push the blue dog down by your feet, then,' he said. 'There isn't room for him up here.'

So Deborah pushed the blue dog down, and Teddy Robinson cuddled beside her and thought how lucky he was not to be just a doll or a hot-water bottle.

Soon the blue dog made the bed so warm and cosy that Deborah fell asleep and Teddy Robinson began to get drowsy. He said, 'Dear me, dear me,' to himself, over and over again; and after a while he began to feel as if he loved everybody in the whole world. And soon his 'Dear me's' turned into a sleepy little song which went like this:

Dear me,
dear me,
how nice to be
as dear
a bear
as dear old me. Dear you, dear him, dear them,
dear we, dear *every* one,
and dear,
      dear
          me.

And then he fell fast asleep.

And that is the end of the story about how Teddy Robinson went to the toyshop.

CHAPTER TWO

TEDDY ROBINSON KEEPS HOUSE

One day Teddy Robinson sat on the kitchen-table and watched every one being very busy. Mummy was cutting bread, Deborah was putting some flowers in a vase of water, and Daddy was looking for a newspaper that had something in it that he specially wanted to read.

Teddy Robinson wished he could look busy too, but he couldn't think of anything to be looking busy about. He stared up at the ceiling. One or two flies were crawling about up there. Teddy Robinson began counting them; but every time he got as far as 'Three' one of them would suddenly fly away and land somewhere quite different, so it was difficult to know if he had counted it before or not.

'What's the matter, Teddy Robinson?' said Deborah.

'Nothing's the matter,' he said. 'I'm busy. I'm counting flies, but they keep flying away.'

'Silly boy,' said Deborah.

'No,' said Mummy, 'he's not silly at all. He's reminded me that I must get some fly-papers from the grocer today. We don't want flies crawling about in the kitchen.'

Teddy Robinson felt rather pleased.

'I like being busy,' he said. 'What else can I do?'

Deborah put the vase of flowers on the table beside him.

'You can smell these flowers for me,' she said.

Teddy Robinson leaned forward with his nose against the flowers and smelled them.

When Daddy had found his newspaper and gone off to work, Mummy put some slices of bread under the grill on the cooker.

'We will have some toast,' she said.

'And you can watch it, Teddy Robinson,' said Deborah.

Just then the front-door bell rang, and Mummy went out to see who it was.

18

Teddy Robinson and Deborah could hear Andrew's voice. He was saying something about a picnic this afternoon, and could Deborah come too?

'Oh!' said Deborah. 'I must go and find out about this!' And she ran out into the hall.

Teddy Robinson stayed sitting on the kitchen-table watching the toast. He could hear the others talking by the front door, and then he heard Mummy saying, 'I think I'd better come over and talk to your mummy about it now.' And after that everything was quiet.

Teddy Robinson felt very happy to be so busy. He stared hard at the toast and sang to himself as he watched it turning from white to golden brown and then from golden brown to black.

In a minute he heard a little snuffling noise coming from the half-open back door. The Puppy from over the Road was peeping into the kitchen. When he saw Teddy Robinson sitting on the table he wagged his tail and smiled, with his pink tongue hanging out.

19

'What's cooking?' he said.

'Toast,' said Teddy Robinson. 'Won't you come in? There's nobody at home but me.'

'Oh, no, I mustn't,' said the puppy. 'I'm not house-trained yet. Are you?'

'Oh, yes,' said Teddy Robinson. 'I can do quite a lot of useful things in the house.'

He began thinking quickly of all the useful things he could do; then he said, 'I can watch toast, keep people company, smell flowers, time eggs, count flies, or sit on things to keep them from blowing away. Just at the minute I'm watching the toast.'

'It makes an interesting smell, doesn't it?' said the puppy, sniffing the air.

'Yes,' said Teddy Robinson. 'It makes a lot of smoke too. That's what makes it so difficult to watch. You can't see the toast for the smoke, but I've managed to keep my eye on it nearly all the time. I've been making up a little song about it:

~ watching the toast ~

'I'm watching the toast.
 I don't want to boast,
 but I'm better than most
 at watching the toast.

'It can bake, it can boil,
 it can smoke, it can roast,
 but I stick to my post.
 I'm watching the toast.'

'Jolly good song,' said the puppy. 'But, you know, it's really awfully smoky in here. If you don't mind I think I'll just go and practise barking at a cat or two until you've finished. Are you sure you won't come out too? Come and have a breath of fresh air.'

'No, no,' said Teddy Robinson. 'I'll stick to my post until the others come back.'

And at that moment the others did come back.

'Oh, dear!' cried Mummy. 'Whatever's happened? Oh, of course—it's the toast! I'd forgotten all about it.'

'But I didn't,' said Teddy Robinson proudly. 'I've been watching it all the time.'

'It was because Andrew came and asked us to a picnic this afternoon,' said Deborah. 'Would you like to come too?'

'I'd much rather stay at home and keep house,' said Teddy Robinson. 'I like being busy. Isn't there something I could do that would be useful?'

'Yes,' said Mummy, when Deborah

asked her. 'The grocery order is coming this afternoon. If Teddy Robinson likes to stay he can look after it for us until we come home. We'll ask the man to leave it on the step and risk it.'

So it was decided that Deborah and Mummy should go to the picnic and Teddy Robinson should stay at home and keep house.

When they were all ready to go, Mummy wrote a notice which said, PLEASE LEAVE GROCERIES ON THE STEP, and Deborah wrote underneath it, TEDDY ROBINSON WILL LOOK AFTER THEM. Then they put the notice on the back-door step, and Teddy Robinson sat on it so that it wouldn't blow away.

Deborah kissed him good-bye, and Mummy shut the back door behind him. Teddy Robinson felt very pleased and important, and thought how jolly it was to be so busy that he hadn't even time to go to a picnic.

'I don't care *how* many people come and ask me to picnics or parties today,' he said to himself. 'I just can't go to any of them. I'm far too busy.'

Nobody did come to ask Teddy

He had a picture in his mind of how he would open the door to the milkman

Robinson to a party or a picnic, so after a while he settled down to have a nice, quiet think. His think was all about how lovely it would be if he had a little house all of his own, where he could be as busy as he liked. He had a picture in his mind of how he would open the door to the milkman, and ask the baker to leave one small brown, and invite people in for cups of tea. And he would leave his Wellington boots just outside the door (so as not to make the house muddy), and then say to people, 'Excuse my boots, won't you?' So everybody would notice them, but nobody would think he was showing off about them. (Teddy Robinson hadn't got any Wellington boots, but he was always thinking how nice it would be if he had.)

He began singing to himself in a dreamy sort of way:

'Good morning, baker. One small
   brown.
How much is that to pay?
Good morning, milkman. Just one
   pint,
and how's your horse today?

'Good afternoon. How nice of you
to come and visit me.
Step right inside (excuse my boots).
I'll make a pot of tea.'

A blackbird flew down and perched on the garden fence. He whistled once or twice, looked at Teddy Robinson with his head on one side, and then flew away again.

A minute later the grocer's boy opened the side gate and came up to the back door. He had a great big cardboard box in his arms.

When he had read the notice he put the big box on the step. Then he picked Teddy Robinson up and sat him on top of it. He grinned at him, then he walked off, whistling loudly and banging the side gate behind him.

The blackbird flew down on to the fence again.

'Was that you whistling?' he asked.

'No,' said Teddy Robinson, 'it was the grocer's boy.'

'Did you hear me whistle just now?' asked the blackbird.

'Yes,' said Teddy Robinson.

'I did it to see if you were real or not,' said the blackbird. 'You were sitting so still I thought you couldn't be, so I whistled to find out. Why didn't you answer me?'

"I'm guarding the groceries"

'I can't whistle,' said Teddy Robinson, 'and, anyway, I was thinking.'

'What's in that box?' asked the blackbird. 'Any breadcrumbs?'

Just then there was a scrambling, scuffling noise, and the Puppy from over the Road came lolloping round the corner. The blackbird flew away.

'Hallo,' said the puppy. 'What are you doing here?'

'I'm guarding the groceries,' said Teddy Robinson.

'Well, I never!' said the puppy. 'You were making toast last time I saw you. You do work hard. Do you have to make beds as well?'

'No,' said Teddy Robinson, 'I couldn't make beds. I haven't got a hammer and nails. But I am very busy today.'

'Why don't they take the groceries in?' asked the puppy.

'They've gone to a picnic,' said Teddy Robinson. 'I stayed behind to keep house. They decided to let the boy leave the groceries on the step and risk it.'

'What's "risk-it"?' said the puppy.

'I don't know,' said Teddy Robinson, 'but I like saying it, because it goes so nicely with biscuit.'

'Got any biscuits in there?' asked the puppy, sniffing round the box.

'I'm not sure,' said Teddy Robinson, 'but you mustn't put your nose in the box.'

'I was only sniffing,' said the puppy.

'You mustn't sniff either,' said Teddy Robinson. 'It's a bad habit.'

'What's "habit"?' said the puppy.

'I don't know,' said Teddy Robinson. 'But it goes very nicely with rabbit.'

Suddenly the back door opened behind him. The puppy scuttled away, and Teddy Robinson found that Deborah and Mummy had come home again.

'You did keep house well,' said Mummy, as she carried him into the kitchen with the box of groceries.

'Don't you think he ought to have a present,' said Deborah, 'for being so good at housekeeping?'

'He really ought to have a house of his own,' said Mummy. 'Look—what about this?' She pointed to the big box. 'You could make him a nice house out of that when it's empty. I'll help you to cut the windows out.'

'Oh, *yes*,' said Deborah, 'that is exactly what he wants.'

So after tea Deborah and Mummy got busy making a beautiful little house for Teddy Robinson. They made a door and two windows (one at the front and one at the back) and painted them green. Then Deborah made a hole in

29

the lid of the box and stuck a cardboard chimney in it. Mummy painted a rambler-rose climbing up the wall. It looked very pretty.

'What would you like to call your house?' said Deborah. 'Do you think Rose Cottage would be a nice name?'

'I'd rather it had my own name on it,' said Teddy Robinson.

So Deborah painted TEDDY ROBINSON'S HOUSE over the door, and then it was all ready.

The next day Teddy Robinson's house was put out in the garden in the sunshine. He chose to have it close to the flower-bed at the edge of the lawn, and all day long he sat inside and waited for people to call on him. Deborah came to see him quite often, and every time she looked in at the window and said, 'What are you doing now, Teddy Robinson?' he would say, 'I'm just thinking about what to have for dinner,' or 'I'm just having a rest before getting tea'.

The Puppy from over the Road came and called on him too. He sniffed at Teddy Robinson through the open

"I never knew there was a house there"

window and admired him more than
ever now that he had a house of his own.

And the garden tortoise came
tramping out of the flower-bed and
looked up at the house, saying, 'Well,
well, I never knew there was a house
there!'

Then the Next Door Kitten came walking round on tiptoe. At first she didn't quite believe it was real. She was sniffing at the rambler-rose painted on the wall when Teddy Robinson looked out of the window and said, 'Good afternoon.'

The kitten purred with pleasure at seeing him.

'What a purr-r-rfect little house!' she said. 'Is it really yours? You *are* a lucky purr-r-rson.'

Teddy Robinson nodded and smiled at her from the window.

'Yes,' he said, 'it's my very own house. Aren't I lucky? It's just what I've always wanted—a little place all of my own.'

And that is the end of the story about how Teddy Robinson kept house.

CHAPTER THREE

TEDDY ROBINSON GOES TO THE WRONG HOUSE

One day Teddy Robinson got left behind by mistake at Auntie Sue's house. He had been there with Deborah and Mummy, and when it was time to go home he was dozing in the rocking-chair, so nobody remembered about him.

When Auntie Sue came back from seeing the others off on the train she found him sitting there all alone.

'Oh, poor fellow!' she said. 'You've gone and got left behind. Whatever shall we do with you?'

Teddy Robinson couldn't think what ought to be done with him, so he didn't say anything.

'I think we'd better post you,' said Auntie Sue. 'I shan't be coming to your house for at least a week, and I'm sure Deborah will want you long before then.'

33

So Teddy Robinson was wrapped in crinkly cardboard and a lot of brown paper, and Auntie Sue tied him up neatly with string. He made a very nice parcel indeed. Then he was taken to the post office and handed over the counter.

Teddy Robinson thought this was the most exciting thing that had ever happened to him. He was longing to get home and tell every one about his adventure, and he thought how jolly it would be to be able to tell a real travel story. He would start by saying, 'When I was travelling by parcel post...' and then every one would say, 'Oh, yes, Teddy Robinson—do tell us about your adventure.'

But it wasn't very exciting after all, because he was so well wrapped up that he couldn't see what was happening to him. Sometimes he seemed to be bumping about in a sack with a lot of other parcels, and sometimes he seemed to be going smoothly along in a car or a train. Then for quite a while he seemed to be just lying somewhere, not moving at all. And it took a long, long

34

time. Teddy Robinson dozed, and woke up, and dozed again.

At last he woke up with a jerk. The noise of a car-engine had stopped, and a chink of light was showing through his brown paper.

'Hooray,' said Teddy Robinson. 'I'm home at last. How surprised Deborah will be to see me!'

But when he was unwrapped Teddy Robinson found that he wasn't at home at all. An old lady was looking at him, and she seemed as surprised as he was.

'Well, now,' she said, 'who ever can you be? And why have you been sent to me?'

She felt all through the wrappings of the parcel and all over Teddy Robinson to see if there was a letter to tell her who he had come from. But there was no letter anywhere. The old lady smiled at him and stroked his fur gently.

'You dear,' she said. 'I wonder who you are.'

Teddy Robinson saw that they were in a garden. The postman must have handed him to the old lady over the front gate, he thought. But why had he

35

come to this house and not to his own house? He couldn't understand it at all. Nor could the old lady.

What had happened was that Auntie Sue had written the number of Deborah's house in a hurry. The number was thirty-nine, but because she was writing it quickly Auntie Sue made the three look like an eight; so Teddy Robinson had been sent to number eighty-nine in his own road instead of number thirty-nine. But he didn't know this. Neither did the old lady.

'I must ask the postman what to do about you next time he comes,' she said.

She began walking slowly up the garden path with Teddy Robinson in her arms. She stopped once or twice to smell a rose, then she sat him down on the front doorstep and went round the side of the house.

Teddy Robinson sat and looked at the garden and thought about how surprised he was to be there.

After a little while the old lady came back wheeling a beautiful big pram. She put it in the middle of the lawn, then she looked up at the sky.

'It's a lovely afternoon,' she said. 'I think the sun's going to be quite hot.'

She let down the hood and fixed a sun-canopy over the pram. It had a long silk fringe round it. Then she turned towards Teddy Robinson and smiled at him, shaking her head.

'I *wonder* who you can be!' she said.

She picked him up and carried him over to the pram. There was a soft woolly blanket inside. The old lady sat him on top of it, then she went indoors again.

'How very kind of her!' said Teddy Robinson to himself. 'I've always wanted to sit in a pram under one of these sunshade things, and this is a fine one. It makes me feel like some one quite important.'

He wished the hedge was low enough for him to see over into the road. He could hear the footsteps of people passing by every now and then, and he thought how pleasant it would be to bow and smile at every one from under the canopy as they passed by.

Soon the old lady came out again, carrying a rug, which she spread on the

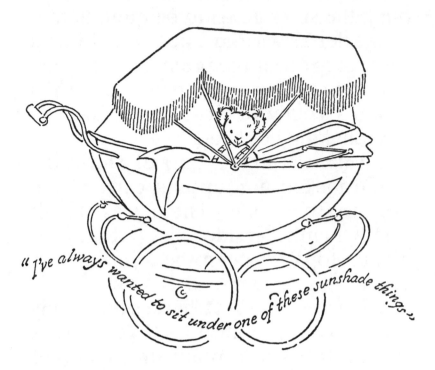

"I've always wanted to sit under one of these sunshade things"

grass close to the pram. As she turned to go back she smiled again at Teddy Robinson and said, 'Now, who can you belong to, you dear old thing? I *do* wonder who you are!'

The old lady said this so many times that after a while Teddy Robinson began wondering too.

I used to be quite sure I was me, he thought, but the old lady doesn't seem to be sure at all. And if I aren't me who

38

am I? I wish Deborah was here to ask.

He began singing to himself, rather sadly, thinking round and round in his head about who he could be,

'If I aren't Teddy R,
then who can I be?
Who can I be
if I aren't really me?

'If I aren't Teddy R,
who every one knows,
I'm some silly bear
who's got lost, I suppose.

'Some silly old bear
just sitting around,
who's nobody's bear
until he gets found.'

'But if I aren't me,' said Teddy Robinson, 'who is going to find me? I don't want to be found by anyone except Deborah. Oh, dear, I wish I'd never gone in a parcel at all.'

Just then the old lady came out again. This time she was carrying a little nursery-table, painted blue, with a chair to match. She set these down on the rug, nodded and smiled at Teddy Robinson, then went indoors again.

'She is going to a lot of trouble for me,' said Teddy Robinson. 'I've always wanted a little chair and table like that. I wonder what she's gone to fetch now.'

Next the old lady brought out a play-pen, and put it by the pram. Teddy Robinson was very pleased.

'I've always wanted a cage like that,' he said, 'so that I could play at being a really fierce bear in the zoo. She *is* a kind old lady.'

After that more and more things were brought out and laid on the lawn. Teddy Robinson grew happier and happier.

There was a big animal picture-book. ('Just the kind I like,' said Teddy Robinson.) There were two deck-chairs. ('One for her and one for me,' said Teddy Robinson, 'but I like the little blue chair best.') And, last of all, a tray of tea-things, and a big iced cake with three candles on it, and the name TEDDY written across the top in pink icing.

"Fancy her even making a cake for me!"

'Well, I never!' said Teddy Robinson.
'Fancy her even making a cake for me!'
He began singing a little song about all
the nice things the old lady was bringing
out into the garden.

'A chair and a table,
painted blue,
a very nice cage
and a picture-book too,

41

a very nice cake,
a very nice pram—
what a very nice bear
she must think I am!'

Just then Teddy Robinson heard more
footsteps coming down the road. Then
suddenly his fur went all tingly with
excitement. He heard Deborah's voice!

They must be coming to fetch me, he
thought, and was very pleased to think
he was found at last.

But suddenly he began to feel rather
shy and silly.

'They'll wonder whatever I'm doing
here,' he said, and decided he would
pretend not to notice them just yet. So
he stayed sitting in the pram without
moving, waiting until they were near
enough to see him.

The footsteps stopped on the other
side of the gate; then Deborah's voice,
sounding very surprised, said, 'Mummy!
Isn't that Teddy Robinson?'

'It can't be, darling,' said Mummy.

'But he's got Teddy Robinson's
trousers on. Look!'

'*Has* he?' said Mummy. 'Are you sure?'

"Isn't that Teddy Robinson?"

They came nearer and peered over the gate. Teddy Robinson stared hard at nothing, with his thinking face on.

'It *can't* be him,' said Mummy. 'How could he have got here? We left him at Auntie Sue's.'

'But it's terribly like him,' said Deborah. 'I didn't think there could be

43

another bear in the whole world that looked so like Teddy Robinson. I wish I could be sure.'

'Oh, dear!' said Teddy Robinson to himself. 'If even Deborah isn't sure I'm me perhaps I aren't me after all.' And he began wondering all over again about who he could possibly be if he wasn't Teddy Robinson.

Deborah looked up at the windows. Nobody was looking, so she opened the gate quietly and ran on tiptoe across the grass to the pram. She looked closely at Teddy Robinson with her head on one side, then she said, 'You *are* Teddy Robinson, aren't you?'

'Oh, I hope I am!' said Teddy Robinson. 'But I've had such a funny, bumpy, all-over-the-place sort of time just lately that I can't be sure of anything. If only you were sure I could be sure too. I do hope I'm me, and not just any old bear.'

Deborah touched his ear gently with one finger.

'You *are* Teddy Robinson,' she said. 'I knew you were! I can see Mummy's stitches where she sewed your ear on.'

She ran back to Mummy, leaving Teddy Robinson where he was.

'It *is* him!' she cried. 'Can I go and take him?'

'No,' said Mummy, 'we'd better not do that. You stay and talk to him while I go and ask.'

So Mummy went up to the house and knocked at the door, and Deborah stayed on the other side of the gate and smiled at Teddy Robinson, and told him over and over again how pleased she was to see him.

'I feel rather sorry for the lady who lives here,' said Teddy Robinson. 'She thinks I've come to stay and she's done such a lot for me. Look at this beautiful pram. She got it specially for me. And look at my beautiful cage over there, and my little chair and table—just what I've always wanted. And do you know— she's even made me a great big cake with three candles on it, and my name written on it in pink icing!'

Mummy and the old lady came down the garden path, laughing and talking together. Just as they were beginning to tell Deborah all about how Teddy

45

Robinson had come by parcel post a taxi drew up at the gate.

'Oh, this will be my family!' cried the old lady. 'You must stay and meet them. They've been away for a week. I've been so lonely without them.'

A little boy got out of the taxi, followed by a lady with a baby in her arms.

'This is Teddy, my little great-grandson,' said the old lady. 'He is three years old today. You must all stay to tea, and help us eat the birthday cake.'

So, after Mummy had said, 'I don't feel we should . . .' and the old lady had said, 'Oh, do,' a great many times, they all sat down to tea in the garden. The baby was put in the pram, and the little boy sat in the blue chair. Teddy Robinson sat inside the play-pen and pretended to be a wild bear, but he was too happy to look very fierce.

They had a lovely tea-party. When it was time to go home the old lady said, 'I hope you will all come again—Teddy Robinson too.' And Deborah said, 'Thank you very much. We will.'

As they walked up the road to their

own house again Deborah said, 'Dear Teddy Robinson, I'm so glad you've come back. It's been horrid without you.'

'Yes, hasn't it?' said Teddy Robinson. 'And wasn't it lucky those children came to stay with the old lady just when they did? She won't miss me nearly so much now. The baby can use my pram, and the little boy can have my chair. It was very kind of her to give me all those nice things, but I'd *much* rather be found again and know I really am Teddy Robinson.'

And that is the end of the story about how Teddy Robinson went to the wrong house.

CHAPTER FOUR

TEDDY ROBINSON'S CONCERT PARTY

One day Teddy Robinson was lying on his back in front of the fire with Deborah's cousin Philip. Suddenly Philip tickled him in the tummy and said, 'I say, Teddy! Let's make a surprise. I feel like doing something funny.'

'Oh, so do I!' said Teddy Robinson. 'Where's Deborah?'

'She's gone to ask Andrew and Mary Anne to tea today,' said Philip. 'Let's think of something to do when they come.'

'I suppose I couldn't have another birthday party?' said Teddy Robinson.

'No,' said Philip. 'We must think of something new. Couldn't we do some tricks?'

'I know!' said Teddy Robinson. 'Ask them to sit down to listen to a story, and then when they're all waiting you just fly out of the window. That would be a jolly good trick!'

'But I can't fly,' said Philip.

'Oh, no. Bother! We can't do that then.'

'Think of something else,' said Philip.

'Make faces at them,' said Teddy Robinson.

'That wouldn't be funny enough to make them laugh.'

'The face you're making now would make anyone laugh,' said Teddy Robinson.

'I'm not making a face. This is my ordinary one.'

'Well, it's different from usual,' said Teddy Robinson.

'That's because I'm thinking. Don't be silly.'

'Well, then,' said Teddy Robinson, 'don't let's try to be funny. Let's do something Sweet and Beautiful and a little bit Sad, like the Babes in the Wood.'

'No,' said Philip. 'Let's have something jolly, even if we can't be funny. Think again.'

'*I* know!' said Teddy Robinson. 'I'll

have a concert party!'

Philip thought this was a fine idea. When Deborah came back he and Teddy Robinson told her all about it.

'I'm going to sing songs,' said Teddy Robinson, 'and say pieces of poetry, and we'll have some refreshments, and then I'll do conjuring tricks.'

'But what's Philip going to do?' asked Deborah.

'Help *me*,' said Teddy Robinson. 'It's *my* concert party.'

'And are you going to make the refreshments too?'

'No,' he said, 'you know I can't do that; but you're going to be very kind, like you always are, and ask Mummy.'

Mummy said, yes, she would make the refreshments. They could have raisins (six each) and chocolate biscuits (cut in halves) and dolly mixtures (handed round in a bowl).

Philip began making the programme, and Teddy Robinson sat beside him and told him what to write. Deborah brought the dolls out of the toy-cupboard and tidied them up.

'You can be the audience,' she said.

Teddy Robinson told him what to write

The stage was a great trouble, until Mummy had a good idea.

'Why not turn the kitchen-table on its side?' she said. 'You can have it in here, just for the afternoon.' She gave them some old curtains and a bunch of chrysanthemums.

'The flowers aren't very fresh,' she said, 'but you might use them for decoration. And you can hang the curtains on a string and tie the ends to the table-legs.'

While Philip and Deborah got the stage ready Teddy Robinson sat thinking hard about all the things he was going to do.

'Are you sure you don't want anyone else to do anything?' asked Deborah. 'It's rather a lot for one.'

'No, thank you,' said Teddy Robinson; 'but I might have Jacqueline in one scene. Is Mary-Anne bringing her?'

(Jacqueline was Mary-Anne's beautiful doll.)

'Yes,' said Deborah, 'and Andrew is bringing his toy dog, Spotty. You might like to use him too?'

'No,' said Teddy Robinson. 'He argues too much.'

When Mary-Anne and Andrew arrived, with Jacqueline and the spotted dog, they found the stage all set up ready. The curtains were hung on a string across the front, and the bunch of flowers hung from the middle, just where the curtains met. (You will see in the picture how it looked.)

In front of the stage all the dolls were sitting in tidy rows, staring at the curtains, and waiting for the show to begin. A large notice was pinned to the door. It said:

TEDDY ROBINSON'S CONCERT PARTY

Programme

RECITATION, by Teddy Robinson

A SEEN FROM SLEEPING BEAUTY, by Teddy Robinson and Jacqueline (thought of by Teddy Robinson)

SONG, by Teddy Robinson

REFRESHMENTS, thought of by Teddy Robinson, handed round by Deborah, made by Mummy

CONJURING TRICKS, by the FAMOUS WIZARD T. NOSNIBOR (helped by Philip)

Audience arranged by Deborah
No smoking or shouting

Jacqueline was very surprised when Mary-Anne told her that she was going to be on the stage. She hadn't been able to read the programme herself, because her eyes were shut.

53

'I'm afraid they're stuck again,' whispered Mary-Anne to Deborah. 'Will it matter?'

'Not a bit,' said Deborah. 'She's going to be the Sleeping Beauty.'

Jacqueline was hustled behind the stage to where Philip and Teddy Robinson were waiting.

'You're on next,' Teddy Robinson told her. 'I'm first.'

'We're ready to begin now,' said Philip.

'About time, too,' said the spotted dog, who was rather cross at not being asked to go on the stage as well.

'Hush!' said all the dolls. 'They're going to begin.'

Teddy Robinson came to the front of the curtain. He bowed low to the audience, then he said:

'Welcome.

'Ladies and gentlemen,
what a sight
to see you sitting here tonight!
I'm pleased to see you
every one,
so clap your hardest when I've
     done—'

54

He bowed low to the audience.

This wasn't really the end of the poem, but as every one started clapping their hardest straight away Teddy Robinson leaned back against the curtain and waited for them to finish. But he had forgotten there was nothing behind the curtain, so a moment later he fell through and disappeared out of sight.

A scene from Sleeping Beauty

The audience didn't know this was a mistake. Every one clapped harder than ever, so nobody heard Teddy Robinson saying, in a rather cross voice, 'But I haven't finished yet! There's another verse.'

'Never mind,' said Philip. 'Let's do the next scene.'

Teddy Robinson's head came out from between the curtains.

'The next scene is Sleeping Beauty,'

(thought of by Teddy Robinson)

he said, 'and please don't clap *till the end.*'

After a little waiting Deborah pulled the curtains aside. This was the first time the audience had seen the whole stage, and every one said, 'Oo-oh, isn't it pretty!'

On a pink cushion lay Jacqueline, fast asleep and looking very beautiful. There were two or three ferns in pots, arranged to look like trees, and some leaves from the garden were sprinkled about on the ground. On the other side stood the wooden horse, and on his back, looking very proud and princely, sat Teddy Robinson. He was wearing the dolls' Red-Riding-Hood cloak (with the hood tucked inside), and a beret with a long curly feather (from one of Mummy's old hats) on his head. He also had a sword (cut out of cardboard) and socks rolled down to look like boots.

'How handsome he is!' said all the dolls.

'Huh!' said the spotted dog. 'I think he looks soppy.'

The horse began to move slowly across the stage towards Jacqueline. Philip was pulling it on a string from the other side; but the string hardly showed at all, so it looked very real. The dolls all wanted to clap, but they remembered just in time and didn't. The horse, with Teddy Robinson on its back, moved slowly forward until its front wheels came up against the edge of the pink cushion. Then it gave a jerk, and Teddy Robinson fell headlong over its neck and landed beside Jacqueline, with his nose buried in the cushion.

Every one waited to see what was going to happen next, but nothing happened. They went on waiting. At last Teddy Robinson said, in a muffled, squeaky voice, 'It's the end. For goodness sake, clap! I'm suffocating.'

Deborah pulled the curtains quickly, and the audience clapped hard.

After a good deal of whispering behind the stage Teddy Robinson's head came out again from between the curtains.

'Ladies and gentlemen,' he said, 'as you never seem to know when it's the end of anything I'll tell you when to clap next time. The next scene is "The Bear in the Wood." '

His head disappeared, but shot out again a moment later.

'You can clap now while you're waiting,' he said.

When the curtains parted once more Jacqueline and the cushion had gone, but the leaves and ferns were still there. Teddy Robinson sat under the largest fern. He began singing:

> 'I'm a poor teddy bear,
> growing thinner and thinner.
> I haven't any Deborah
> to give me any dinner.'

The audience loved this. They laughed loudly, because Teddy Robinson looked so very fat and cosy that they thought he was trying to be funny. But Teddy Robinson had meant it to be a sad song. He went on:

> 'I'm lost in a wood
> where the trees are thick and high.
> If some one doesn't find me
> I might lie down and die.'

'Oh, dear!' said one of the dolls. 'Let me find him! I think he means it.'

Teddy Robinson turned to the audience and said:

> 'I hope you won't get worried
> at this sad, sad song.
> I'm lying down to die now,
> but I shan't stay dead for long.'

60

He then lay down in the middle of the stage, and Philip emptied a basketful of leaves over him. Teddy Robinson sang the last verse,

'With only leaves to cover me
and grass beneath my head,
that is the end of the Bear in the Wood,
and now I'm really dead. You can clap now.'

The audience clapped and cheered. Some of them thought it was sad, and some of them thought it was funny, but they all loved it. After that it was time for the refreshments.

Philip and Teddy Robinson, behind the curtains, were busy clearing away the leaves and ferns.

'How is it going?' whispered Teddy Robinson.

Philip peeped through the curtain.

'I think it's going jolly well,' he said. 'They seem to be enjoying the refreshments like anything.'

When all was ready, and the last raisin had been eaten, Deborah drew the

61

The Famous Wizard Nosnibor

curtains for the Famous Wizard Nosnibor.

Teddy Robinson was sitting in the middle of the stage. He had a tall white paper hat on his head, and another hat (one of Daddy's) lay on a little table beside him.

'Why is he wearing a dunce's hat?' asked the spotted dog in a loud voice.

'He isn't,' whispered Deborah. 'It's a

wizard's hat.'

'Hush!' said all the dolls. 'He's going to begin.'

Philip handed him a stick covered with silver paper.

'This is my magic wand,' said Teddy Robinson in a deep voice, 'and I am the famous Wizard Nosnibor.'

Then he waved the wand over the hat on the table, and said:

'Abracadabra,
titfer-tat.
You'll find a rabbit
inside the hat!'

Philip lifted up the hat, and there, underneath it, sat Deborah's stuffed rabbit. All the dolls clapped and said:

'What a wonderful trick!'

But the spotted dog said, 'I know how he did that one. He put the rabbit there before we started.'

'Hush!' said the dolls. 'He's going to do another trick!'

Philip put two little bowls on the ground in front of Teddy Robinson. One was red and the other was white.

He turned them both upside down, then he put a marble under the red bowl.

'Which bowl is the marble under?' said Teddy Robinson.

'The red one,' everybody shouted.

Teddy Robinson.waved his magic wand over the two bowls and said:

> 'Roll, little marble,
> roll, roll, roll.
> Choose for yourself
> your favourite bowl.'

'Oh, *I* know that trick!' shouted the spotted dog. 'I saw a man do it at a party. The marble's gone under the other bowl, the white one. *That's* not a new trick!'

Teddy Robinson waited, looking mysterious and important. Philip lifted up the white bowl. There was nothing there. Then he lifted up the red bowl. There was the marble!

'You see,' said Teddy Robinson, 'it *is* a new trick.'

The dolls clapped even harder and cried, 'Oh, *isn't* he clever!'

But the spotted dog kept saying, over and over again, 'It *wasn't* a new trick. Look here, listen to me—'

'Andrew,' said Deborah, 'if you can't keep Spotty quiet I think you'd better take him away.'

'Oh, all right,' said Andrew. 'I'll keep him quiet.'

'Now,' said Teddy Robinson, 'if you've all finished clapping I'll show you my next trick.'

'*I* wasn't clapping,' said the spotted dog.

'This trick,' said Teddy Robinson, 'is called The Magic Flowers.'

Philip laid a small bunch of flowers on the left-hand side of the stage. Teddy Robinson waved his magic wand and said,

'Snip-snap-snorum, fiddle-de-dee, hokum-pokum, one-two-three. Magic Flowers on the floor, come to Wizard Nosnibor!'

The bunch of flowers began moving slowly across the floor all by itself. The audience clapped and cheered.

Teddy Robinson waved his magic wand once more, and then the biggest and best surprise of all happened. The bunch of chrysanthemums hanging above his head suddenly fell straight down into his lap, and at the same minute the curtains fell down on top of him, covering everything except his nose and one eye. The audience cheered louder than ever.

Teddy Robinson said, 'THE END,' very slowly and loudly, and bowed beneath the curtains.

There was a great deal of noise after this. The audience was still clapping and cheering, and Philip was shouting, 'Hooray for the Famous Wizard!' And Mary-Anne was telling everybody it was the nicest concert party she had ever seen. Only Spotty was still arguing.

'I don't believe there *is* such a person as the Wizard Nosnibor,' he said.

'If some people could read other people's names backwards,' said Teddy Robinson, 'they wouldn't think they were quite so clever.'

Much later on, when it was all over, Deborah said, 'Teddy Robinson, that *was* a lovely concert party!'

'Yes, wasn't it?' said Teddy Robinson.

'Do tell me how you did the Magic Flowers,' said Deborah.

'A piece of black cotton was tied on to them,' said Teddy Robinson. 'Philip pulled it.'

'But how did you get the other flowers and the curtains to fall down at exactly the right minute?'

'I'll tell you a secret,' said Teddy Robinson. 'I didn't. I think the string broke. You couldn't have been more surprised than I was. Don't tell anyone, will you?'

And this is the end of the story about Teddy Robinson's concert party.

CHAPTER FIVE

TEDDY ROBINSON GOES TO THE DOLLS' HOSPITAL

One day Teddy Robinson was waving good-bye to Daddy when he waved so hard that all of a sudden his arm came right off.

'Oh, my goodness,' he said, very surprised to see his arm in Deborah's hand without the rest of him joined on to it, 'I seem to be going all to pieces.'

'Never mind, my poor boy,' said Deborah; 'Mummy will mend it.'

But Mummy said she could only sew it on, and then it wouldn't be able to swivel round any more.

'And what's the good of that?' said Teddy Robinson. 'I *must* have an arm that swivels round.' And he was so set on it that Mummy said he had better go to the Dolls' Hospital.

So off they went to the toyshop, which was also the Dolls' Hospital. Teddy Robinson was so pleased to be

"—and when are visiting days, please?"

going that he sang all the way there, and
Deborah hardly had a chance to remind
him about saying please and thank you,
and not showing off, and not singing
too loudly in the middle of the night.

The man in the Dolls' Hospital said
yes, he could mend Teddy Robinson's
arm and they could fetch him again on
Friday.

'This is his nightie,' said Deborah,
handing a little bag over the counter,
'and when are visiting days, please?'

'Oh, dear,' said the man; 'I don't usually have visiting days. People just come when it's time to fetch them again.'

Deborah was rather disappointed. She had hoped she would be able to see all the dolls in their little cots and beds.

'It doesn't seem fair,' she said. 'He came with me when I went to hospital.'

But the man promised to take good care of him, and as he looked the sort of man who understood teddy bears, Deborah decided not to mind and kissed Teddy Robinson good-bye.

After that he was taken into a room behind the shop where all the other animals and dolls were waiting to be mended. The man put him up on the top shelf between a stuffed horse and a felt cat; then he went back to the shop.

The stuffed horse looked at Teddy Robinson. He lowered his head; his legs slipped out sideways.

'Horsey's the name,' he said. 'How do you do? No need to ask why you're here—I see you've lost an arm, poor fellow.'

'Oh, no, I haven't lost it,' said Teddy

70

"My trouble's of long standing"

Robinson; 'I've brought it with me. It just needs fixing on again.'

'My trouble's of long standing,' said the horse. 'You see, it's my legs. They slide out sideways and then I fall on my nose. I'm hoping to get new wires put in them.'

The felt cat stared hard at Teddy Robinson as if she wanted to be noticed. He smiled politely.

'I hope you are not here for anything serious?' he asked.

'It's my insides,' said the cat, smiling proudly. 'My squeak is worn out. They're going to put a new one in, *if* they can, which I very much doubt.' She purred softly. 'I'm not at all an easy case.'

'Oh, I'm sorry,' said Teddy Robinson.

'*I* don't mind,' said the cat. 'It's very interesting. Makes something to talk about. I like coming here.'

'Have you been here before, then?'

'Oh, yes, often. There's nothing I haven't had done—new ears, new eyes, re-stuffing, everything.'

'Fancy that,' said Teddy Robinson, 'and I thought I was quite important coming only once.'

The dolls all made quite a fuss of Teddy Robinson because he was the only teddy bear there. They called him Teddy right from the start, so he decided not to bother about his second name as he didn't want to make himself seem more special than anyone else.

And then the Other Bear arrived. He was a new-looking bear with golden-yellow fur, and when he was brought in all the dolls said, 'Oooh, what a handsome teddy bear! Shall we call him Goldie?'

But the Other Bear said, 'No, thank you. I prefer to be called by my own

name. It is rather a distinguished one.'
He then bowed slightly from the waist,
looking very proud and handsome, and
said, 'You may call me Teddy
Robinson.'

'Hi!' called Teddy Robinson from the
top shelf, 'you can't do that. It's my
name.'

'Oh, no,' said the felt cat, 'you can't
have it too. He thought of it first—a
most distinguished name.'

'You can have Brown for a second
name,' said one of the dolls kindly. 'It
will suit you.'

So from then on Teddy Robinson was
called Teddy Brown, and the Other
Bear was called Teddy Robinson, which
made the real Teddy Robinson very
cross indeed.

The dolls made as much fuss of the
Other Bear as they had made of Teddy
Robinson. He told them he was there
because one of his legs was loose,
although he was still almost new.

'I was expensive,' he said, 'so it
should never have happened. I think it's
because I've been shown off so much.
I'm rather a special bear, you see. I'm

told some one has even written a book about me.'

'You *are* lucky to be such a Special bear,' said the dolls.

'Oh, yes,' said the Other Bear, 'but I suppose we can't all be Special, and I expect even quite ordinary bears with names like Smith or Brown have people who are quite fond of them.'

Just then the shop man came in, carrying a beautiful big doll. She was wearing a pink silk dress with a bonnet to match and she had a very pretty face. But her eyes were closed.

Teddy Robinson looked over the top shelf and saw that it was Jacqueline. Jacqueline was a doll he knew. She belonged to a little girl called Mary Anne who was a friend of Deborah. Teddy Robinson had always admired Jacqueline ever since she had come to his birthday party and laughed at all his jokes. Her eyes had been shut even then, but she had never stopped smiling all through the party.

The shop man laid Jacqueline down gently on the bottom shelf, next to the Other Bear, then he went out again.

'Oooh!' said all the dolls. 'A Sleeping Beauty!'

Jacqueline smiled sweetly, then said, 'Tell me, is my friend Teddy Robinson still in the hospital?'

'Why, yes!' they said, 'he is right beside you.'

Up on the top shelf the real Teddy Robinson was doing his best to fall at Jacqueline's feet and tell her that *he* was the real one.

'Stop pushing,' said the horse. 'You'll only upset everybody. We don't all want to fall off the shelf'

'But I know her!' said Teddy Robinson.

'Why all the fuss?' said the felt cat. 'Can't somebody ask her if she knows Teddy Brown?'

'Teddy Brown?' said Jacqueline, 'no, I've never heard of him.'

'There you are, you see,' said the felt cat, 'she doesn't know you at all. It's Teddy Robinson she knows, and I'm not surprised—such a distinguished name. Now do sit quiet.'

So poor Teddy Robinson had to sit tight while the others talked down

75

below.

'I've come to have my eyes unstuck,' he heard Jacqueline say. 'They were shut even when I came to your party, do you remember?'

'No, I can't say I do,' said the Other Bear, who, of course, hadn't been at Teddy Robinson's party at all.

'Who is that growling up there?' asked Jacqueline suddenly.

'Teddy Brown,' said the dolls. 'Take no notice.'

'What a bad-tempered bear,' said Jacqueline. Then she said to the Other Bear, smiling sweetly, 'Don't you really remember me, Teddy Robinson?'

'No, I'm afraid not,' said the Other Bear, 'but of course I meet so many pretty dolls I could hardly remember them all.'

'I never thought Teddy Robinson would forget me,' said Jacqueline sadly. 'I always remember him and how beautifully he sang.'

'Yes,' said the Other Bear, 'I am told I have quite a good voice—a sort of bearitone,' and he began making a sort of growling la-la-la noise.

'Are you *sure* you're Teddy Robinson?' said Jacqueline, looking puzzled. 'You sound so different.'

'Of course I'm sure,' said the Other Bear.

'And yet,' said Jacqueline, 'Teddy Robinson used to make up proper songs, with his own words, not just la-la-la.'

'All right, so can I,' said the Other Bear, and after a lot of coughing and humming and ha-ing he sang:

'I—er—ah—um, here's a song
all about er—um—ah—um,
hear me sing—er—sing a song,
la-la-la-la tumty-tum.'

'No,' said Jacqueline, 'you're not Teddy Robinson at all. I didn't think you could be. Teddy Robinson is not only the handsomest and cleverest bear I know. He is also the most modest. And he would never call *that* singing.'

Up on the top shelf the real Teddy Robinson was thinking round and round in his head. He had been quite sure he was Teddy Robinson until he heard Jacqueline say what a bad-tempered bear he was. Then he began to wonder.

'How can I be sure I'm me?' he asked the horse quietly.

'Who else do you feel like?' said the horse in a horse whisper.

'Well, I'm not feeling quite myself,' said Teddy Robinson, 'but I thought it was having only one arm.' He began singing softly:

'Am I me?
 Or am I me?
 And if I'm not,
 who can I be?'

'I know that voice!' cried Jacqueline, down below.

'It's the silly bear on the top shelf,' said the dolls.

'Do let him go on,' said Jacqueline, and when Teddy Robinson heard this he knew that of course he was himself, even if he didn't *feel* quite himself, and he sang out at the top of his voice:

'Stick me up
    or blow me down,
    call me Smith
    or call me Brown,
    call me Jones
    for all I care,
    call me just a silly bear,
*but I'm still Teddy Robinson and
nobody else, so there!'*

And then, because he had no breath
left, he overbalanced, and with a cry of
'Jacqueline!' he fell at her feet with a
bump.

'Oh, my dear Teddy Robinson, is it
really you?' she said. 'I'm so glad! Who
ever is this silly Other Bear who's been
calling himself you?'

All the others began talking at once,
saying, 'Fancy that,' 'The Other Bear
took his name,' 'What a shame!' but
Teddy Robinson and Jacqueline hardly
heard them, they had so much to say to
each other.

As for the Other Bear, he never said
a word, but just sat up straight and
proud, pretending not to notice, until
the shop man came in and fetched him

"Jacqueline!" he cried, and fell at her feet

away to be mended.

After that it was Teddy Robinson's turn. When his arm had been fixed on again the man pinned a label on him and carried him into the shop. There on the counter sat the Other Bear, also with a label on, all ready to go home.

The man put them down side by side,

but the two teddy bears took no notice of each other. Each of them was trying hard to read the other one's label without looking. Then all of a sudden they both looked very surprised indeed.

'I say!' said Teddy Robinson, 'is that your label?'

'Yes,' said the Other Bear. 'Is that yours?' For both the labels had Teddy Robinson written on them.

'I say, I'm awfully sorry,' said Teddy Robinson. 'I'd no idea there was anyone else in the world with the same name as me. You must have had rather

"*I say! Is that your label?*"

a horrid time in there with every one thinking you were pretending to be me. No wonder you were so quiet.'

'Least said soonest mended,' said the Other Bear, 'and I *was* soonest mended.'

'So you were,' said Teddy Robinson. 'But I am sorry.'

'I thought you were making it up,' said the Other Bear. 'After all, Robinson is such a distinguished name. I'm surprised at *you* having it.'

They were still both busy being surprised when the shop man came back, carrying a big telephone book.

'They asked me to phone when this one was ready,' he said to his wife, 'and now I've gone and lost their number.' He turned over the pages. 'Hmmm,' he said, 'just as I thought, pages and pages of Robinsons. Why, there must be more than a thousand of them. I'll never find the right one.'

He went away again, scratching his head.

'Pages and pages of Robinsons?' said Teddy Robinson. 'Well, bless my braces!'

'*And*,' said the Other Bear solemnly, 'if even half of those Robinsons have teddy bears it means there must be about four-hundred-and-ninety-nine other Teddy Robinsons, besides me.'

'What about me?' said Teddy Robinson.

'You're just one of the four-hundred-and-ninety-nine other ones,' said the Other Bear.

'Well, blow me up and stick me down, I think I'll change my name to Brown,' said Teddy Robinson.

But at that minute the shop door opened and in came Deborah and Mummy. Teddy Robinson forgot all about changing his name to Brown, and all about all the other Teddy Robinsons, he was so pleased to see them.

Deborah hugged him and admired his mended arm.

'How does it feel to have two again?' she asked.

'Fine,' said Teddy Robinson, swivelling it round as fast as it would go. 'I got so used to having only one that it felt like having two, so now I've got two it feels more like three. I only need one more and I shall feel like a windmill.'

Just then Deborah saw the Other Bear on the counter.

'*Look*, Mummy!' she said. 'It's another Teddy Robinson.'

'Why, so it is!' said Mummy.

'How funny that such an ordinary-looking bear should have our name,' said Deborah.

'Well, ours is a very ordinary name,' said Mummy, laughing. 'There must be hundreds of Teddy Robinsons, when you come to think of it.'

'But only one really Special one like mine,' said Deborah, hugging him all over again.

And that is the end of the story about how Teddy Robinson wvent to the Dolls' Hospital.

CHAPTER SIX

TEDDY ROBINSON AND THE CHINA GNOME

One day Teddy Robinson and Deborah were looking at the marigolds and radishes coming up in their garden when the postman came by with a big parcel for Deborah. On one side it had a label which said FRAGILE. HANDLE WITH CARE.

'Now, what can that be?' said Deborah, and she ran indoors with it and sat Teddy Robinson down on the table so that he could watch while she opened it.

'Fragile. Handle with care,' said Deborah. 'I wonder what it is.'

'It's got a beautiful name,' said Teddy Robinson. 'I wish my name was Fragile, but of course I haven't got a handle.'

'No, it isn't a name,' said Deborah, 'and it doesn't mean it's got a handle. It means it's precious and mustn't be dropped or kicked around in case it gets

85

broken.'

'Ah,' said Teddy Robinson, and he began singing:

'Fragile, fragile
Teddy R.,
what a precious bear I are.
Never leave me on the ground
in case I'm squashed or kicked
around.
Fragile, fragile—'

'Don't be silly,' said Deborah, 'you aren't fragile. I expect this is some kind of ornament, that's what.'

'Well, I shall be called Fragile too,' said Teddy Robinson. 'I shall have it for my second name.'

Deborah pulled off the brown paper and opened the box, and there inside, among a lot of straw shavings, she found a china gnome sitting on a china toadstool. He had a bright blue jacket, a pointed red hat, and a long white beard.

'Oh, how sweet!' she said. 'I believe it's an ornament. And there's a letter here too, it says "love from Uncle

86

Michael". I must go and show Mummy.'
And off she ran.

'An Ornament,' said Teddy Robinson
to himself several times over. 'An
Ornament. It sounds rather an
important thing to be. More important
than Bear or Cat or Dog,' and he began
wondering what it was that made an
ornament an Ornament, and not just
something ordinary.

Deborah came running back.

'Yes,' she said. 'it *is* an ornament.
Aren't I lucky? I've had lots of toys, but
I've never had an ornament of my own
before. I shall keep it here always,' and
she put it on the end of the
mantelpiece, next to Daddy's pipe-rack.

'But that's where I sit,' said Teddy
Robinson.

'Only sometimes,' said Deborah. 'You
can sit anywhere because you're a teddy
bear. Ornaments have to go on the
mantelpiece because they're fragile.'

'Well, that settles it,' said Teddy
Robinson. 'I'll be Fragile too. If he sits
in my place, then I'll sit in his box. Do
you mind lifting me in, very carefully?'

So Deborah lifted him into the box,

Teddy Fragile Robinson.

and Teddy Robinson sat among the straw shavings and felt very precious indeed.

He began singing a little song about it:

'Fragile is my middle name,
handle me with care,
Teddy Fragile Robinson,
the ornamental bear.'

But just then Mummy called to Deborah to bring the box out into the kitchen, because she didn't want the straw shavings all over the carpet. So Teddy Robinson was lifted out again, and that was the last he saw of the box.

He sat on the table and looked up at the china gnome. It wasn't a very friendly looking ornament, but he thought he had better be polite, so he said, 'I hope you're comfortable up there? You get a nice view of everything, being so high up, don't you? I often sit there myself.'

The china gnome didn't even turn his head, but said in a cracked and crusty voice, 'I'm surprised they let you sit up here. The mantelpiece is the place for ornaments, not for toys. I am a very precious and fragile ornament.'

'Well, I'm not exactly a toy,' said Teddy Robinson. 'I am a very precious and fragile teddy bear. I don't wind up or run about on wheels, so you wouldn't exactly call me a toy.'

'Oh, yes, I would,' said the china gnome. 'A soft toy, that's what you are, and you ought to be kept in the toy cupboard. That's the place for soft toys.'

'*Nothing*,' said Teddy Robinson loudly.

'What do you mean?'

'What I say. Deborah's always told me that if I can't think of a polite answer it's better to say nothing. So that's what I said.'

After that he was quiet for a long while because he was thinking all over again about what it was that made an ornament an Ornament, and not just something ordinary.

'Why are you staring at me like that?' said the china gnome.

'I was wondering what it is you've got that I haven't,' said Teddy Robinson.

'You haven't got a beard, or a pointed hat.'

'No, you're right. I wonder I didn't think of it.'

When Deborah came back again Teddy Robinson said, 'Would you be so kind as to make me a pointed hat?'

'Yes, if you like,' said Deborah, and she made him one out of newspaper.

'And now would you get some cotton

90

wool and some string?'

'What ever for?' said Deborah.

'To make me a beard,' said Teddy Robinson.

So Deborah fetched them, and she did just as Teddy Robinson told her, and put a big lump of cotton wool over the lower part of his face, and tied it round his head with a piece of string.

'Now put me on the mantelpiece,' he said, 'and tell me how many ornaments you see there.'

Deborah stood back and looked at the mantelpiece.

'I see the clock,' she said, 'and Daddy's pipe-rack, and one china ornament, and my dear old teddy bear, with cotton wool all over his face and a paper hat on.'

'Oh,' said Teddy Robinson, 'you're quite sure I don't look like an ornament?'

'Quite sure,' said Deborah, laughing. 'You look rather funny, really.'

'All right,' said Teddy Robinson. 'Take them off again. There's no point in making a fool of myself for nothing.'

Deborah had just taken them off

'You're quite sure I don't look like an ornament?'

again when there was a ring at the
doorbell, and a moment later in came
Andrew. He admired the china gnome
very much, and Deborah told him all
about how it had come when she and
Teddy Robinson were in the garden.

'And that reminds me,' she said, 'my
radishes are nearly ready to be picked.
Come and see.'

'I'll just fetch Spotty in,' said Andrew,
'I left him in the hall.'

Spotty was Andrew's toy dog who usually came with him when he came to play with Deborah. Teddy Robinson didn't care for him much because he always wanted to argue, so he quickly put on his Thinking Face and pretended to be making up poetry.

Andrew put them side by side in the arm-chair.

'They can talk to each other while we're busy,' he said.

When the others had gone the spotted dog stared hard at the gnome with his black boot-button eyes, and said rudely, 'That's new. What is it?'

'It's an ornament,' whispered Teddy Robinson.

'Ah, yes, of course. Very useful things, ornaments,' said the spotted dog, who always knew everything.

'What for?' asked Teddy Robinson.

'For being ornamental, of course,' said Spotty.

'Oh,' said Teddy Robinson. 'Yes, of course. What does ornamental mean, exactly?'

'It's what ornaments are,' said Spotty. 'Surely you knew that?'

'Yes,' said Teddy Robinson. 'Of course. I don't know why I asked.'

'Nor do I,' said Spotty. He then stared hard at the china gnome again and barked rudely, 'Hey, Mister Ornament! How do you like living with a teddy bear who doesn't know what ornamental means?'

The china gnome said, in a sharp, cracked voice, 'I don't like it at all. Neither do I like being shouted at by a rude dog who ought to be outside in a kennel.'

The spotted dog looked very surprised.

'This place seems more like a zoo than a house,' said the china gnome. 'You ought to be outside in the garden.'

'Oh, no,' said Teddy Robinson, 'Spotty isn't a real dog, he's a real *toy* dog; same as I'm not a real bear, but a real *teddy* bear.'

'Then he ought to go in the toy cupboard too,' said the gnome.

There was a rustling noise at the open window, and the Next Door Kitten jumped up on the sill.

'Hallo,' she purred, when she saw

94

Teddy Robinson in the chair. 'Are you coming out?'

'Not just now,' said Teddy Robinson, 'but won't you come in?'

'Thank you,' said the Next Door Kitten, and she jumped through the window and landed on the arm of the chair.

'Who's the old gentleman on the mantelpiece?' she whispered through her whiskers.

'*That*,' said the spotted dog in a loud, rude voice, 'is the ugliest, nastiest—'

But Teddy Robinson said quickly, 'Sssh! He's an ornament. He's come to live here.'

The Next Door Kitten jumped lightly on to the mantelpiece and picked her way carefully along to the china gnome.

'Miaou do you do?' she said politely. 'What purrrfectly lovely weather we're having.'

'Get down! Get down at once!' snapped the china gnome. 'How dare you get up here?'

The Next Door Kitten stepped back, surprised.

'But I often come up here,' she said.

95

'I come to talk to Teddy Robinson when he's sitting up here.'

'Well, he's not going to sit up here any longer,' said the gnome. 'I don't like my sitting-room cluttered up with a lot of soft toys. I'm going to arrange for him to live in the toy cupboard. It isn't as if he were an ornament. As for you, get down at once and go back in the garden where you belong. I won't have wild animals in my room.'

'But it's not your room,' said the Next Door Kitten, 'it's Teddy Robinson's, and he invited me in.'

'Yes, I did!' shouted Teddy Robinson from the armchair, 'but I never invited you. You just came in a parcel without being asked. I've tried to be polite to you and make you feel at home. I've let you sit in my place on the mantelpiece, but all you've done is be rude to me and my friends, so now I'm not going to try to make you feel at home any more. A gnome in the home is a terrible bore, and I don't want a gnome in my home any more. I shall ask Deborah to have you taken away.'

He stopped for breath; then he said,

"You just came in a parcel without being asked."

'If I wasn't so angry I'd make a song about it. I nearly did by mistake.'

Just then they heard footsteps outside. The Next Door Kitten turned quickly, brushing against the china gnome by mistake, and jumped down off the mantelpiece. At the same minute the china gnome fell with a thud on to the carpet.

No one spoke. The Next Door Kitten jumped out of the window, and sat washing her paws quietly on the ledge outside, as if nothing had happened. Then Teddy Robinson peered over the edge of the chair to see what had happened to the china gnome. He was still all in one piece, but there was a long crack down one side of his blue china jacket.

'Poor thing,' said Teddy Robinson kindly, 'I'm afraid you're cracked.'

'Mind your own business,' said the china gnome, and his voice sounded crustier and more cracked than ever. 'I don't talk to soft toys.'

'Well, I may be soft,' said Teddy Robinson, 'but I'm glad I'm not cracked.'

Then the door opened and in came Deborah and Andrew.

'Oh!' said Deborah, 'my ornament has fallen down!'

'And it's cracked down one side,' said Andrew.

'Never mind,' said Mummy, coming in after them, 'it won't show when he's in the garden where he belongs.'

'In the garden?' said Deborah, surprised.

'Yes,' said Mummy, 'he's a garden

ornament. Didn't you read Uncle Michael's letter?'

'Oh, no, I forgot!' said Deborah. 'It was such grown-up writing. But I thought he'd sit on the mantelpiece.'

'Oh, no,' said Mummy, 'I don't think he'd look right in here at all, but he'll be lovely in your garden.'

'Oh, yes! He can look after the plants!' said Deborah.

'And frighten the birds away,' said Teddy Robinson.

'Like a scarecrow,' said the spotted dog.

So the china gnome was taken out and put in Deborah's garden, all among the radishes and marigolds, where he really looked quite pretty. Then Deborah found Uncle Michael's letter and read it aloud to Teddy Robinson. It said:

Dear Deborah,

I hope you will like this little gnome for your garden. I think his name must be Grumpy because he looks rather cross, so he may be useful for frightening the slugs and

99

earwigs away. I didn't buy you an indoor ornament because of course you have always got Teddy Robinson.

Love from,

UNCLE MICHAEL

'I think that is a very sensible letter,' said Teddy Robinson. 'I always did like Uncle Michael. Can I sit on the mantelpiece again now?'

'Of course,' said Deborah, and she lifted him up.

'There's just one thing more I want to know,' said Teddy Robinson. 'What exactly *is* an ornament?'

'Why, you funny old boy,' said Deborah. 'Surely you knew that? It's something you put on a shelf because it looks pretty.'

'Well, fancy that!' said Teddy Robinson. 'Then I've been an Ornament all along and I never knew.'

And that is the end of the story about Teddy Robinson and the china gnome.

CHAPTER SEVEN

TEDDY ROBINSON GOES UP A TREE

One day Deborah said to Teddy Robinson, 'Mary Anne is coming to play today, and she's bringing Jacqueline.'

'Hooray,' said Teddy Robinson. Jacqueline was his favourite of all the dolls he knew, and he hadn't seen her since they had been in the Dolls' Hospital together.

'Have her eyes been mended?' he asked.

'Yes,' said Deborah, 'and Mary Anne says she is looking more beautiful than ever.'

'What colour are they?' asked Teddy Robinson.

'I forgot to ask,' said Deborah. 'Blue, I expect. I like blue.'

'Or pink,' said Teddy Robinson. 'I like pink, and they would match her dress.'

riding Deborah's tricycle

without his paws on the handlebars

And he looked forward to seeing Jacqueline, with her eyes open at last, in the beautiful pink silk dress and bonnet that she always wore.

While Deborah ran down to the shops to buy some dolly mixtures for them all to share, Teddy Robinson sat in the garden and thought about what he might be doing when Jacqueline arrived.

'It would be nice,' he said to himself, 'if she should just happen to come along when I just happened to be doing something that just *happened* to be rather clever or special or grown-up. Not on purpose, of course, but just if it happened to happen that way.'

And he began wondering whether he might perhaps be swinging from a tree by only one arm, or riding Deborah's tricycle without his paws on the handlebars, or striding up and down the garden in his wellington boots, pushing a wheelbarrow, like the gardener.

But I can't swing from a tree even with two arms, he thought, and I can't ride a tricycle, and I haven't got any wellington boots, so none of those things will do. I must think again.

He had just decided that perhaps it would be best if he was found reading a grown-up book (without any pictures) and humming a little tune to himself (to show it was quite easy) when Timmy White came into the garden.

Timmy White belonged to Mrs White, the lady who sometimes came to help with the cleaning, and he had

or striding up and down the garden in his wellington boots, pushing a wheelbarrow

come out into the garden hoping to find Deborah. But Deborah was still out, and as Timmy White was a very shooty, shouty, bang-bang-bang sort of boy, Teddy Robinson thought it better just to stay quiet and hope he wouldn't be noticed.

Timmy White ran up and down the lawn, making fierce machine-gun noises with his mouth, and shooting at people who weren't there till they were all dead. Then he picked up a ball and threw it so far that it went right over the wall. After that he galloped all the way round the garden, picking things up and throwing them down again, until he came to where Teddy Robinson was sitting. Then all of a sudden, before he had time to say a word, Timmy White had picked him up and thrown him high into the air.

Up and up went Teddy Robinson, higher and higher, and then—swish!— he fell right into the middle of the apple-tree. A sea of green leaves brushed his face as he began falling again, and then suddenly he stopped with a jerk and found himself sitting astride a branch.

When he was quite sure he had stopped falling Teddy Robinson looked down through the leaves and saw that he was still a long way up from the garden. In the distance he could see Timmy White running away into the house.

'Well, I never,' said Teddy Robinson. 'Fancy him doing that. And fancy me finding myself here. I seem to have happened on to this branch without quite knowing how. What you might call an Oblivious Coincidence.'

'Goodness, what a shock you gave me!' chirped a bird, peering down from above with frightened eyes. 'I'm all of a flutter.'

'I do beg your pardon,' said Teddy Robinson; 'but I've just been the Victim of an Oblivious Coincidence.'

'What does that mean?' said the bird.

'I don't know,' said Teddy Robinson. 'I've just made it up, but they're jolly long words, aren't they, and I've just come a jolly long way up. I've never been as high as this in my life before.

'I'm higher than you,' said the bird.

'I dare say you are,' said Teddy Robinson, 'but you don't have to get down again. I do.'

'Shall I push you with my beak?' said the bird, flapping its wings.

'Oh, no, don't do that!' said Teddy Robinson, and his voice went up into a squeak. 'Do stop flapping. You make me feel all wobbly. Just tell me what you would do if you were me—there's a good bird.'

'But that's just what I should do,' said the bird. 'I should flap my wings to stop myself falling.'

'But I haven't any,' squeaked Teddy Robinson.

The bird flew down a little way and looked at Teddy Robinson's furry arms carefully.

'Try flapping those,' he said. 'They'd probably do as well.'

'But I seem to need them for holding on with.'

'Well, you can't have it both ways,' said the bird. 'You can't expect to hold on and fly at the same time.'

'No, I suppose I can't,' said Teddy Robinson. 'Perhaps I'll just hold on for now, and think about flying later.'

The bird flew down beside him and began hopping up and down on the branch.

'Bounce a bit,' he said. 'It's quite fun, especially when the wind's blowing like it is now.'

'Ooo-err, look out!' said Teddy

Robinson, as the branch waved up and down under him.

But it was all right. He seemed to be stuck quite firmly where he was, and after a while he stopped feeling wobbly, and began to enjoy himself instead.

'This is very jolly,' he said, bouncing a little higher. 'I've never been so high up in the world before. I should think I'm jolly nearly at the top of the tree. It's making me feel quite bouncy. I always knew I was a clever bear, but I'd no idea I was as clever as this, to be sitting right up here all by myself. Why, anybody'd think I'd climbed up here just for fun. What a very clever bear I are! It really is very jolly getting above myself like this.' And he began singing:

> 'Three cheers for me
> at the top of the tree,
> the cleverest bear you ever did see.
> Nobody knows
> how clever I are.
> Who would suppose
> I could climb so far?
> Three cheers for me

"Three cheers for me at the top of the tree."

at the top of the tree.
Oh, what a wonderful bear I be!'

Just then he heard voices, and, peeping down, Teddy Robinson saw Deborah searching about at the foot of the tree.

'That's funny,' she was saying. 'Where's Teddy Robinson? I'm sure I left him here. He was waiting to see you. He couldn't have walked off all by himself.'

'Goodness, they must have come already!' said Teddy Robinson. And then he suddenly remembered this was just what he'd wanted. To be found doing something rather clever and grown-up as if it was the easiest thing in the world. So he stared up into the branches, and said in rather a loud voice, 'What a wonderful view one gets from up here!' Then he bounced gently up and down again in the wind, and began singing to himself in an airy sort of way:

'Easy-peasy, pudding and pie,
easy as pie
to climb so high.
The view from here
at the top of the tree
is just the thing
for a chap like me.
Easy as pie,
why don't you try?
Easy-peasy, pudding and pie.'

There was silence for a moment. Teddy

Robinson peeped down with one eye and saw Deborah staring up at him through the leaves as if she could hardly believe her eyes.

'Easy as pie,' he said again.

'Teddy Robinson!' said Deborah. 'What ever are you doing up there?'

'Oh, just looking around,' said Teddy Robinson, in a light, careless sort of voice. 'Have our visitors arrived?'

'Yes,' said Deborah, 'but what have you been *doing*?'

'Doing? Well, I've been bird-watching, as a matter of fact.'

'Bird-watching? But how did you get up there?'

'How did I get up here? Oh. I—er— I just happened to be thinking about something, and then before I knew where I was I happened to find myself here. Just like that.'

Deborah looked as if she didn't believe it, so Teddy Robinson went on, 'You know how easy it is, if you're thinking about something else, to fall down by mistake. Well, if you happen to be thinking about something rather important, as I was, I suppose you

111

might just happen to fall up instead of down, mightn't you?'

Deborah didn't say anything, she was still so surprised.

'—if you forgot to notice which way you were going, I mean,' said Teddy Robinson.

But Deborah wasn't listening any more.

'Oh, dear, oh, dear!' she was saying. 'How shall we get him down?'

'Ask your mummy; perhaps she's got a ladder,' said Mary Anne.

'Oh, yes,' said Deborah, and they ran off into the house, leaving Jacqueline on the rug at the foot of the tree.

'Oh, Teddy Robinson!' said Jacqueline, gazing up to where she could just see the ends of his legs, 'I never dreamt I should find you doing anything quite so wonderful as climbing a tree. What a very clever bear you are!'

Teddy Robinson was just going to say, 'Yes, aren't I?' but he remembered in time, and said instead, 'Oh, it's nothing really. It passes the time and makes a change.'

'I do hope they'll be able to get you

down soon,' said Jacqueline. 'Did you know my eyes were mended?'

'Yes, I am glad,' said Teddy Robinson. 'I've been looking forward to seeing you with them open.'

'And I've been looking forward to seeing *you* with them open,' said Jacqueline. 'It will be the first time.'

Teddy Robinson suddenly went very quiet up in the tree. He had forgotten that Jacqueline would now be able to see him. He looked down at his short, fat legs with their worn brown fur and his shabby trousers, and began thinking very hard, trying to remember what he had told her about himself.

'Er—Jacqueline, did I ever tell you how big I was?'

'Oh, yes, Teddy Robinson, lots of times!'

'Oh!'

He thought for another minute; then he said, 'And how big, exactly, was that?'

Jacqueline laughed. 'What a funny question!' she said. 'As big as you are, of course.'

'Perhaps I'm not quite so big as you

thought I meant I was,' said Teddy Robinson. 'I mean I might look smaller now.'

'Of course you won't,' said Jacqueline. 'Why should you? Teddy bears don't shrink.'

'No,' said Teddy Robinson, 'but the funny thing is I am beginning to feel rather small. It's come on quite suddenly. I feel as if I'm getting smaller and smaller every minute.'

He was quiet for a little while, then he called down again. 'Jacqueline, what sort of color did I tell you my fur was?'

'Didn't you say it was a soft golden brown?'

'Did I?' said Teddy Robinson unhappily. 'Oh, dear, I hope I didn't, because now I come to think of it I don't think it is a very golden brown. I think it's more what you'd call a sort of brownish brown. And there isn't a lot of it.'

Jacqueline laughed again. 'You are a funny bear, Teddy Robinson. Why should you want to make yourself sound so plain and ordinary, when I know you're not?'

'Well, it's just come to me that perhaps I am rather plain and ordinary after all,' said Teddy Robinson. 'Much plainer and ordinarier than I thought I was a little while ago.'

'I don't believe you,' said Jacqueline.

'But you must believe me!' said Teddy Robinson. 'Listen, I can hear them coming. Please let me tell you quickly what I'm really like,' and he began gabbling very fast. 'I'm a plain and ordinary family bear, not very dark and not very fair, a brownish brown, with brownish eyes, and only a *middling* kind of size. My ear came off a while ago, it's mended now but the stitches show, my fur's worn thin with too much kissing, one of my braces' buttons is missing, and—'

But before he could say any more the others had come back. Mummy was with them, carrying a long stick with a feather duster on top of it. She poked about among the branches saying, 'That naughty Timmy White must have thrown him up here. Ah, here he is!' and a moment later Teddy Robinson went tumbling through the leaves to

—*felt smaller than ever.*

the ground.

Deborah picked him up and brushed the twigs off him, and Mummy said, 'Well, he doesn't seem any the worse for his adventure,' and went back to the house. Then he was put to sit on the rug beside Jacqueline while Deborah and Mary Anne shared out the dolly mixtures on to dolls' plates.

Teddy Robinson stared hard at the worn brown fur on his short, fat legs and felt smaller than ever. It seemed such a silly sort of come-down for someone who'd been at the top of a tree, to be poked down on the end of a feather duster.

But when at last he looked up he saw that Jacqueline was smiling at him, and her eyes were big and blue and shining.

'Oh, Teddy Robinson,' she said, 'you look just how I've always imagined you! I knew you were big and brave and handsome, but I did hope you didn't look proud. And you don't. I'm so glad. I think it's so important that brave and splendid people should look kind and cosy as well, don't you?'

And that is the end of the story about how Teddy Robinson went up a Tree.

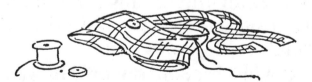

CHAPTER EIGHT

TEDDY ROBINSON IS A POLAR BEAR

One day Teddy Robinson sat under the apple-tree looking at a picture book. A little wind rustled the branches over his head, and soon one or two leaves came fluttering down around him.

'Dear me,' said Teddy Robinson, looking upward, 'this tree seems to be wearing out. Its leaves are falling off.'

Then the wind blew a little stronger and one or two pages blew out of the book (which was an old one) and fluttered away on to the grass.

'There now,' said Teddy Robinson, looking after them, 'this book seems to be wearing out too. It's losing its leaves as well.'

The wind blew stronger still, rustling the leaves and bending the long grass sideways.

'Br-r-r-r!' said Teddy Robinson: 'it's cold. The wind's blowing right through my fur.'

'It's getting thin,' said a sparrow, flying past. 'You should have chosen feathers like me. They wear better.'

'Good gracious, do you mean I'm wearing out too?' said Teddy Robinson. But the sparrow had gone.

The garden tortoise came creeping slowly past.

'I'm quite worn out myself,' he said. 'I've been tramping round and round looking for a nice warm place to go down under. This pile of leaves looks as good as anywhere. Are you coming down under too, teddy bear? Winter's coming soon and the nights will be growing cold.'

'Oh, no,' said Teddy Robinson, 'I always have a nice warm place down under Deborah's blankets when it's cold at nights.'

'Oh, well, here goes,' said the tortoise, and he began burrowing, nose first, deep into the pile of leaves.

'Anyway,' said Teddy Robinson to himself as he watched the tortoise disappear, 'I wouldn't care to spend the winter down there. Besides, I can't quite remember what it is, but I believe there's something rather nice happens in winter-time. Something worth staying up for.'

So the tortoise stayed buried, and the wind blew colder, and more and more leaves fell off the apple-tree. And because it had grown too cold to play in the garden any more, Teddy Robinson and Deborah played indoors or went for walks instead.

Then one day Teddy Robinson looked out very early in the morning, and saw that all the garden was white with snow. There was snow on the trees, and snow on the roofs of the houses, and thick snowflakes were falling in front of the window. He pressed his nose against the glass and stared out.

'Goodness gracious me,' he said, 'some one's emptied a whole lot of white stuff all over our garden. How different it looks!'

A robin flew down from a near-by tree, scattering snow as he flapped his wings. He hopped on to the windowsill and looked at Teddy Robinson through the window with his head on one side.

"Good morning! What do you think of this?"

'Good morning!' he chirped. 'What do you think of this? Got any crumbs?'

Teddy Robinson nodded at him behind the glass and said, 'Good morning. I'm afraid I haven't any crumbs just now, but I'll ask Deborah at breakfast-time. What's it like out there?'

'Lovely,' said the robin, puffing out his red waistcoat. 'But you wouldn't like it. Snow is all right for white polar bears, but not for brown indoor bears. Well, I must be off now. Don't forget my crumbs!'

He flew away, and Teddy Robinson went on watching the snowflakes falling outside the window and sang to himself:

'There's snow in the garden,
 and snow in the air,
 and the world's as white
 as a polar bear.'

When Deborah woke up, Teddy Robinson showed her the snow as proudly as if he had arranged it all himself (it felt like his snow because he had seen it first), and she was very pleased. As soon as breakfast was over she put out a saucer full of crumbs on the sill (because he had told her about the robin), and then she put on her coat and boots.

'I'm going to be very busy now,' she said. 'Andrew and I are going to dig away all the snow from people's gates.'

as proudly as if he had arranged it all himself.

'Can I come?' said Teddy Robinson.

Deborah looked out. 'Yes,' she said,.
'it's stopped snowing now. You can sit
on the gate-post and watch us.

So Deborah and Andrew started
clearing the snow away from all the
front gates while Teddy Robinson sat
on his own gate-post and watched them.
And after a while it began to snow

again. Teddy Robinson got quite excited when he saw the big snowflakes settling on his arms and legs, and he began singing again, happily:

'There's snow in the garden,
and snow in the air,
and the world's as white
as a polar bear.

Snow on the rooftop,
and snow on the tree,
and now while I'm singing
it's snowing on me!'

'Hooray, hooray,' he said to himself. 'Perhaps if it snows on me long enough I shall be all white too. I should love to be a polar bear.'

And it did. It snowed and snowed until Teddy Robinson was quite white all over, with only his eyes and the very tip of his nose showing through.

'I don't believe even Deborah would know me now,' he said, chuckling to himself. And it seemed as if he was right, because when Deborah came running back for dinner Teddy

Robinson kept quite still and didn't say a word, and she ran right past him into the house without recognizing him.

'This *is* fun!' said Teddy Robinson. 'All this snow must be the nice thing I'd forgotten about, that happens in winter-time. It was worth staying up for.' And he felt sorry for the poor old tortoise who was down at the bottom of the pile of leaves and missing it all.

How surprised Deborah will be when she comes back and finds I've turned into a polar bear, he thought.

But Deborah didn't come back because after dinner she made a snowman in the back garden and forgot all about him. Teddy Robinson didn't know this, but he was having such a jolly time being a polar bear all by himself on top of the gate-post that he didn't notice what a long time she was.

First the Next Door Kitten came picking her way along the wall, shaking her paws at every step. She looked at Teddy Robinson as if she didn't quite believe in him, and they had a little conversation.

'Who are you?'

'I'm a polar bear.'

'Why aren't you at the North Pole?'

'I came to visit friends here.'

'Oh!'

Then Toby the dog (who belonged to Deborah's friend Caroline) came galloping up. He was a rough and noisy dog who liked chasing cats and barking at teddy bears. The Next Door Kitten jumped quickly over the wall into her own garden, but Teddy Robinson kept quite still until Toby was sniffing round the gatepost. Then he let out a long, low growl.

Toby jumped and barked loudly. Teddy Robinson growled again.

'Who's that?' barked Toby.

'Gr-r-r, a polar bear. Run like mad before I catch you!'

Toby looked round quickly, but couldn't see anyone.

'Go on, *run*,' said Teddy Robinson in his big polar bear's voice. 'RUN!'

Toby didn't wait for any more. With a yelp which sounded more like Help! he ran off up the road as fast as he could go.

'Well, I'll never be frightened of *him*

again,' said Teddy Robinson.

Then the robin flew down from the hedge and perched on the gate-post beside him and cocked a bright eye at him.

'Hallo,' he chirped. 'Who are you?'

'I'm a polar bear.'

The robin looked at him sideways, hopped round to his other side, and looked again. Then Teddy Robinson sneezed.

'You're not,' said the robin. 'You're the brown bear who lives in the house. I saw you this morning. I told you then this snow isn't right for an indoor bear like you. You'll catch cold. But thanks for my crumbs. I'll look for some more at tea-time. I hope you'll be having toast? I like toast.' And before Teddy Robinson could answer he had flown off again over the white roofs of the houses.

It grew very quiet in the road. People's footsteps made no sound in the snow and it seemed as if the world was wrapped in cotton wool. Teddy Robinson was beginning to feel cold. Soon one or two lights went on in the houses, and in a window opposite he could see a lady getting tea ready.

'I wonder if she is making toast,' he said to himself, and felt a little colder.

Then he began thinking about the tortoise tucked away in the big pile of leaves.

'He must be quite cosy down there,' he said, and he thought of the leaves all warm and crunchy and smelling of toast, and almost wished he had gone down too.

'But of course, if I had, I should never have been able to be a polar bear sitting on a gate-post,' he said; and to keep his spirits up he began singing a polar bear song:

> 'Ice
> is nice,
> and so
> is snow.
> Ice
> is nice
> when cold winds blow—'

but the words were so cold that they made him sneeze again.

'Never mind,' said Teddy Robinson bravely, 'I'll think of something else. I'll make up a little song called The Polar Bear on the Gate-Post.'

But it was hard to find anything to rhyme with gatepost, and the more he thought about it, the more he found himself saying 'plate' instead of 'gate', and 'toast' instead of 'post', so that in the end, instead of singing about a Polar Bear on a Gate-Post, he was singing about an Indoor Bear on a Plate of Toast, which wasn't what he'd meant at all.

'But it *would* be nice and warm sitting on a plate of toast,' he said to himself. And then suddenly he thought, Of course! *That's* the nice thing that happens in wintertime. It's not snow at all. It's toast for tea!

And at that moment the robin came flying back chirping, 'Toast for tea! Toast for tea! Is it ready?'

When he found the saucer empty on the windowsill and poor Teddy Robinson still sitting in the snow, with an icicle on the end of his nose, the robin was quite worried.

"—just like a Christmas card—"

'They must have forgotten you,' he said. 'I'll remind them.' And he flew up to the window and beat his wings hard on the glass. Then he flew back to Teddy Robinson.

Deborah came to the window and looked out.

'Oh, Mummy!' she called. 'There's the robin, and he's sitting on—he's sitting on—why, it's Teddy *Robinson*, all covered in snow and looking just like a polar bear! And the robin's sitting on his head.'

'Oh, don't they look pretty!' said Mummy. 'Just like a Christmas card.'

Then Teddy Robinson was brought in and made a great fuss of. And afterwards, while Mummy made the toast for tea and Deborah put out fresh crumbs for the robin, he sat in front of the fire and bubbled and mumbled and simmered and sang, just like a kettle when it's coming up to the boil:

'Tea and toast,
  toast and tea,
  the tea for you
  and the toast for me.
  How nice to be a warm, brown bear
  toasting in a fireside chair.'

When bedtime came Teddy Robinson's fur was still not quite dry, so Mummy said he had better stay downstairs and she would bring him up later. So

Deborah went off to bed, and Mummy went off to cook grown-up supper, and Teddy Robinson toasted and dozed in the firelight and was very cosy indeed.

Then Daddy came home, puffing and blowing on his fingers and stamping the snow off his shoes. He took a little parcel out of the pocket of his big overcoat and gave it to Mummy. Inside was a fairy doll, very small and pretty, with a white-and-silver dress, and a silver crown and wand.

'Oh, a new fairy for the Christmas-tree!' said Mummy, standing her upon the table. 'How pretty! That is just what we need. Now come and have supper, it's all ready.'

So Daddy and Mummy went off to their supper, leaving the fairy doll on the table and Teddy Robinson in front of the fire.

'A new fairy for the Christmas-tree,' said Teddy Robinson to himself. 'The *Christmas-tree*. I'd forgotten all about it,' and his fur began to tingle. He suddenly remembered how the Christmas-tree looked, with toys and tinsel all over it, and little coloured lights, and a pile of exciting little parcels all round it. And he remembered himself, sitting close beside it in his best purple dress, trying to see if any of the parcels were for him, without looking as if he was looking. And then he remembered how there always was a parcel for him, and how it was always just what he wanted.

'Of course!' he said, *'that's* the nice thing that happens in winter-time, that I'd forgotten about. It's not snow (though that's very nice), and it's not toast for tea (though that's nicer still), but it's Christmas, and that's nicest of all!'

There was a rustling over his head and the fairy doll whispered in a tiny little voice, 'Would you like a wish, teddy bear? If you like you can have one now. It will be the very first wish I've ever given anyone.'

Teddy Robinson said, 'Thank you,' then he thought hard, then he sighed happily.

'It seems a terrible waste of a wish,' he said, 'but I don't think I've anything

133

left to wish for. I'll wish you and every one else a very merry Christmas.'

And that is the end of the story about how Teddy Robinson was a Polar Bear.